GNOMETTES
VOLUME 2
GLORIOUS GUARDIANS OF THE GARDEN

Welcome to the amazing world of Gnomettes! In Gnomettes 2: Glorious Guardians of the Garden, you'll meet a group of special gnomettes who protect the Earth and its creatures.

Get ready for an exciting adventure! Open this coloring book and let your imagination take you to a magical garden. Each page is a window into the Gnomettes' world, waiting for your colors to make it come alive. Feel the happiness of creating something beautiful and connect with nature in a special way.

GNOMETTES

VOLUME 2
GLORIOUS GUARDIANS OF THE GARDEN

The pages are single-sided to prevent bleed through.

COMING SOON...

Gnomettes Vol. 3

By Alledras Designs

Made in the USA
Las Vegas, NV
26 November 2023